FOR THE 84

THANK YOU

To my family, thank you for encouraging me in everything I choose to do.

To my friends, you inspired this more than I will ever be able to admit to your faces.
I want to thank you for the struggles that I made it through because you were there
(both the ones you know about and the ones that you don't).

To my old English teachers – this is all your fault.

To the man who I saw standing on the edge of the Tyne Bridge,
I hope you have found peace.

Thank you Erin Keenan-Livingstone for the cover design.

Thank you, all.

TRIGGER WARNING

MESSAGES
TO DEAD BOYS

The communications that you are about to read are entirely fictional.
They do however, represent a reality that is spreading.
If you are struggling, please seek help.

Butterstone Medical Practice

Date: 02/03/19
[PATIENT NO. 334997]

Dear Mr. Spriggs,

This is a letter issued on behalf of Dr. Mayes at Butterstone Medical Practice. After being prescribed a six month course of 60mg Fluoxetine Dr. Mayes would like to arrange a follow up consultation to review your medication. Please find below a list of available dates.

Available Consultation Times:
9th March - 11:45am
12th March - 15:35pm
14th March - 8:45am

Please confirm your selection of appointment via Telephone (020 8712 9378) between the hours of 08:00 and 18:30 on Monday - Friday or alternatively email office@butterstonemedical.com outlining your patient number within the response. Please email if none of these times are suitable.

If you need any urgent medical attention please contact the following phone numbers/website chats or make your way to your local Accident & Emergency.

MIND:
Phone: 0300 123 3393
(Monday to Friday, 9am to 6pm)
Website: https://www.mind.org.uk

Samaritans:
Phone: 116 123
(free 24-hour helpline)
Website: https://www.samaritans.org/

Kind Regards,
Butterstone Medical Practice

22nd February 11:09 AM

Hi mate, how brutal was that meeting today. Felt sorry for you having to take all that chew. I wouldn't worry about it though pal. Everyone knows Simon's a prick.

22nd February 12:34 PM

Meet you in the canteen in 5 pal? Need to talk to you about that thing I mentioned earlier. No biggie, nothing to worry about. Just what Janet from HR heard.

    Aa

 Adam Richards
Active 1 hour ago

7th March 2:04 PM

Simon is an arsehole

12th March 10:34 PM

I wish he'd shut up too. Doesn't stop wittering on from that cubicle does he?

Manager my fucking arse.

 Anyone could do a better job than him

    Aa

14th March 9:13 AM

How long you gonna be mate?

Can't cover for you too much longer

Simon keeps asking questions

 Where are you? You ill? Or just slept in 😂

14th March 9:41 AM

 Be prepared when you come in cause he's
in a proper stinker.

    Aa

14th March 3:04 PM

Fucking hell mate wasn't expecting that.

 What did they end up dragging you in for?
Not you gonners is it?

    Aa

15th March 2019

Dear Mr. Spriggs,

This letter constitutes official documentation and records your attendance at a final disciplinary hearing held in [Meeting Room 2] on 14th March 2019 at 14:00 pm.

As discussed within the meeting you have violated Article 3.5 of your contractual agreement on multiple occasions. The performance of any Hawkstone Ltd. employee must fall within the acceptable standards of behaviour as outlined within Article 3.4 - 3.9 of the working contract.

For the purposes of administration, it must be stated that you refused to be accompanied into the hearing by a colleague, a trade union representative or an official employed by a trade union.

If the standard of your working behaviour does not improve or deviates from those outlined within the company policy, your position at Hawkstone Ltd will be terminated with immediate effect. If you need to view your contractual agreement, you can request a copy from the Human Resources department on the fourth floor or email henry.pickford@hawkstone.co.uk for an electronic copy.

This note will be held in your working case file until 15th March 2020. You have the right to appeal this decision in writing to Henry Pickford within 5 working days of receiving the disciplinary notice.

Sincerely,

Simon Bell

Office Manager

Hawkstone Ltd.

T: +0711 821 6977 ext. 3244
s.bell@hawkstone.com

Mon, Mar 4 2019, 11:23 AM

Did you book an appointment at the Doctors? J x

Thu, Mar 7 2019, 1:44 PM

How's work going? Just on my lunch now. Ring me if it's easier. J x

Sun, Mar 10 2019, 3:36 AM

What you doing up?

Are you coming to bed?

Try not to worry.

Snuggles waiting for you. J x

 iMessage   Send

Tue, Mar 12 2019, 1:22 PM

Will you grab some toilet roll from Tesco please babe?

We're all out

I found out the hard way

Today 10:32 PM

Feel stupid texting you cause you've only gone downstairs to get me a drink but thanks for tonight

Really felt like I had the old you back.

Your spark was there. Pasta was gorgeous.

I love you.

Two sugars. J x

iMessage   Send

PayDayLoans.

Dear Mr. Spriggs,

We note at PayDayLoans.com that the balance of your account has not been paid as contractually agreed. For ease of reference, the invoice of your loan has been attached to this final page of this letter. As listed in the documents that follow you owe a total sum of **£7,937.34**. This payment was due to be paid on the scheduled payment plan dates attached to page 3 of this document.

If you have made a payment towards the balance before receiving this letter, PayDayLoans.com apologises for any inconvenience and thanks you for addressing the matter.

This document is the third attempt of correspondence that has been sent to this address. It is the responsibility of the borrower to update the lender about any personal information changes that arise. If your place of residence has changed please contact Emma West immediately on 01847 883003. For legal reasons, all attempts of communication are also emailed to the customer.

If no attempt of repayment has been made then please contact Ian Donnerton on 01847 883028 within 7 days of receiving this letter to discuss the reasons for not making your scheduled repayments.

Alternatively, please make the full payment of £7,937.34 within 10 working days via one of the methods attached to the invoice.

PayDayLoans.

As three attempts of written contact have been made to the customer; no more forms of communication of this kind will be sent. The next stage involves a face-to-face visit by a third party collection company. During this stage, some goods may be valued and taken from your property as a method of repayment. A charge for this third party service will be added to the outstanding amount.

We will continue to add the daily rate of interest to the balance at £1.34 under the terms of the contractual agreement signed at the start of the borrowing process.

Yours Sincerely,

Alan Serranto
Finance Executive at PayDayLoans.com

Company No: 00092384
Case No: 398579
Registered in England & Wales

Sat, Feb 23 2019, 6:04 PM

Hi mate

How you doing?

A few of us are going out for
Crouchy's birthday next
Saturday if you wanna join?

Fri, Mar 1 2019, 11:23 PM

Good seeing you tonight pal

Fri, Mar 22 2019, 2:44 PM

Fancy a catch up tonight once
you've finished work mate?

Fri, Mar 22 2019, 8:33 PM

Remember pal, I'm here if you
need me at all. You're my best
mate and I know if can be
fucked sometimes. We can get
through it tho pal. Try not to
worry bout stuff. I know that's
easier said than done. But if
you need me, I'm here for you.

I'll send through those Miami
pics I was on about

You're gonna crease

Tue, Mar 26 2019, 5:38 PM

Had a nightmare day at work

Fancy a beer?

It's on me

Wed, Mar 27 2019, 8:04 PM

Get together with the boys on Friday mate

Meal for Jack's 30th at Alexander's

Be just like the good old days

No pressure tho man

I'll add you to the Facebook event anyway

Jane's

JANE'S FLORIST - ORDER CONFIRMATION:#7725

OPENING HOURS

MON – FRI	9:00AM – 4:30PM
SAT	10:00AM – 4:00PM
SUN	CLOSED

#7725

Order Date: 28/03/19

DESCRIPTION	QTY
White Roses	x 1
Red Roses	x 2
Crimson Roses	x 2
Purple Hyacinth	x 2
Lillies	x 3
Gladiolus	x 4

TOTAL	£33.99
DELIVERY	£4.99
SUB TOTAL	£38.98

PAYMENT INFORMATION

Jane's Florist
Account Number: 341507864861762

Thanks!

www.janesflorist.co.uk

TESCO

COULBY NEWHAM
any questions please visit
www.tesco.com/store-locator

WHITE TOILET TISSUE	£2.09
SKIMMED MILK, 2 LT	£0.79
MEAL FOR 2 PROMOTI	£4.99
TORTILLA WRAPS PLA	£0.79
PARACETAMOL	£0.67
PARACETAMOL	£0.67
NAPOLINA, PENNE 500G	£1.00
CHICKEN BREAST FILL	£3.19
PORK SAUSAGES	£2.99

TOTAL	£17.08
CASH	£20.00
CHANGE DUE	£2.92

CLUBCARD STATEMENT
Clubcard Number	***************0515
Qualifying Spend	3.15
Points this Visit	17
Points balance	222

9740 1041 1502 2117 2243 5707 6518 50

A chance to win a £1000 Tesco gift card
and collect 25 Clubcard points.
Visit www.tescoviews.com t's & c's apply

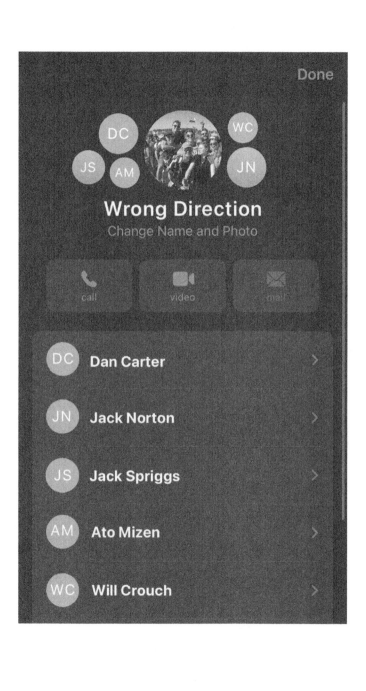

Done

Wrong Direction

Change Name and Photo

call video mail

DC	**Dan Carter**	>
JN	**Jack Norton**	>
JS	**Jack Spriggs**	>
AM	**Ato Mizen**	>
WC	**Will Crouch**	>

Dan Carter

Boys, anyone around?

Will Crouch

What do you want now mate?

Jack Norton

Here he goes, what do you want now Carty?

Dan Carter

Hahahahaha fuck off pal

Jack Norton

Hahah you know were joking pal, whats up?

Dan Carter

Nowt. I was wondering if anyone watched the game?

Jack Norton

Wouldn't watch that shite if you peyd me

Ato Mizen

Nah pal I have better things to be doing with my time hahaha

Mate have you really just spelled paid as peyd. Knew you were dyslexic but fucking hell. That's another level. Hahahaha

Will Crouch

I did Carty. Fulham let me down on my accumulator I was fuming.

Dan Carter

Hahahah how did I know you'd have a bet on

Must be Ladbrokes best customer you

Will Crouch

Don't mate, if Ella finds out I'm fucked

Supposed to be saving for our mortgage aren't I

Jack Norton

Actually how far are you under that thumb?

Hahahah joking, I get it man. I hate adult life. Can't we go back to being 16 when Dan was obsessed with trying to finger every girl in year 12

Dan Carter

Hahahah fuck off

Wish it was a lie tho

I was obsessed

Will Crouch

Hahahah nah, we all were mate. It was only Spriggsy who wasn't cause he was actually fingering the sixth form girls

Sun, Mar 17 2019, 7:49 PM

Will Crouch

Always been a lucky lad
haven't you Spriggsy

Dan Carter

The man, the myth and very
much the legend. Jack
Sprigssssyyy

Jack Norton

Anyone spoken to the fella
recently? He's in this chat isn't
he?

Will Crouch

Yeah he's in it. Must just never
read it. The twat. Must be too
busy for us boys now
hahahaha

B&Q
Middlesbrough 1286
Cleveland Retail Park, Skippers Lane, Mi
TS6 6UB
01642 430043
Email:Middlesbrough.DutyManager
@b-and-q.co.uk
45 Days Returns Policy
See Overleaf

1x   DIALL JUTE ROPE 35X24
5010212627242
                              £2.79

1x   MIRROR GANJI CURVED BLACK
5023076022153
                              £16.00

2 Item(s)

TOTAL   £18.79

Card sale
************9425

Visa Debit   CONTACTLESS
Number: ************9425
Auth Code: 456116
AID: A0000000031010
App Date:
App Seq No: 00 Issue:
Merchant ID: ##34999
Terminal ID: ####7383
Permanent TID: 31493120
Reference: 0268 1286 128601

Please debit my account

NO CARDHOLDER VERIFICATION

RT128612860122022102S847

Transaction in accordance with notified
terms and conditions.

lease retain for your records.

Wed, Feb 27 2019, 11:08 AM

HI LUVVIE, THIS IS MY NEW NUMBER

MUM..X

Wed, Feb 27 2019, 11:34 AM

Didn't meant the capitals...Sorry luv. Just figuring out this new phone

Mum x

Fri, Mar 1 2019, 6:49 PM

Do you want to come over for tea one night this week?.

Mum x

Sat, Mar 9 2019, 6:11 PM

Hello?...Are you coming over?

We can rearrange if you are busy darling...I'll give your tea to the dog

He will luv it lol.

Mum x

iMessage   Send

TESCO

COULBY NEWHAM
any questions please visit
www.tesco.com/store-locator

	£12.25
MARLBORO CIGARETTES	£1.99
MOTHER'S DAY CARD	£18.00
JACK DANIELS OLD NO.7	
	£32.24
TOTAL	

CARD STATEMENT
************0515

Card Number   32.24
Qualifying Spend

* PAYMENT VOID *

9740 1041 1502 2117 2243 5707 6518 50

Notifications

Q

Earlier

 Daniel Carter invited you to 'Jack's 30th birthday'. Respond to let them know if you can attend.
•••
2 h

 It's **Richard Hanalo**'s birthday today. Let him know that you're thinking about him!
•••
13 h

 It was **Lauren Jackson**'s birthday.
•••
5 d

 Debrah Wiles changed her profile picture.
•••
1 w

 Toni Fitzharris and **Freddie Atkinson** liked your comment "Happy Birthday TF!🎈 ".
•••
1 w

 Daniel Carter replied to your comment.
•••
1 w

Wed, Mar 20 2019, 8:22 PM

Lovely seeing you tonight darling...x Your Dad checked and it was A. France + Son solicitors that we used...Why do you need them??? Is it for the house? Or something for you and Jess??

X

Also...have a bloody shave luv. You looked scruffy 2day. lol x.

Are you coming over next Thurs? I'll go and get fish and chips...it can b our early Mothers Day xX

Sun, Mar 31 2019, 8:20 AM

Thanks for the flowers. They're gorgeous. Love you x

Mum x

Tue, Mar 19 2019, 6:49 PM

This clearly isn't working out. It's been holding me down for weeks now and I just don't know what to do anymore Jack. I know that you're not in the best place babe and I know that it's hard for you. I try and be there, I do. But its starting to get to me too. I don't think that what we have is going to work until you sort yourself out. Thats horrible of me to say and I hate to do it but drinking, the argument, mood swings. It's not good for either of us. You know I love you, I do. But its taking its toll on me.

If you need more help, can you please check back in with the doctors and just see what else they can do? I know they weren't the best last time but things are changing everyday and they might be able to offer you something that works. I know work are hounding you too, but you can always look for other jobs. I'll get Aaron to read over your CV if you want. The pressure can't be nice and I know it gets to you but you can't always be moody with me because of it. I just want us to be how we used to be.

I'm moving to my Mum's for a few days. Just so that we have some space from one another. I'm not saying this is the end of us at all. I'm not. But we need a break for a bit. Sort yourself out for me this time. I love you.

Q Search mail

☐ ▾ C ⋮

☐	Primary	⚎ Social	🏷 Promotions
☐ ☆	INDEED	Are you sick of your job? Want a new one? Find o
☐ ☆	Spotify	Cancellation Request: #97229 - Are you sure you
☐ ☆	Trainline	Get our free app for live train times.
☐ ☆	MR PORTER	The latest for Mr. Spriggs: your style update for to
☐ ☆	PureGym	Pure Gym cancellation policy states that you must
☐ ☆	Amazon.co.uk REVIEWS	Jack Spriggs, did you enjoy 'Alan Watts: Wisdom
☐ ☆	NETFLIX	How To Cancel Your Account: Was It Something W
☐ ☆	Just Eat	Jack, Get 15% off tonight's dinner...
☐ ☆	PayDayLoans	FINAL WARNING - Dear Mr. Spriggs...
☐ ☆	Twitter	What's happening near you

Fri, Mar 8 2019, 4:09 PM

How much you wanting?

📞 PHONE
+44 7590817 - - -
Missed call

📞 PHONE
+44 7590817 - - -
Duration 1 min 33 seconds

Fri, Mar 8 2019, 9:32 PM

Behind the garage near Tesco

📷 iMessage   Send

IMDb Top 250 - IMDb   www.imdb.com

someone saved my life tonight elton john - YouTube   www.youtube.com

Home | Mind   www.mind.org.uk

10 Things You Can Do to Boost Self-Confidence   www.entrepreneur.com

Disruption of Serotonin Contributes to Cocaine's Effects | National Institute on Drug Abuse (NIDA)

cocaine effect on brain - Google Search   www.google.com

Fluoxetine (Prozac): an antidepressant - NHS   www.nhs.uk

Causes of Depression: Genetics, Illness, Abuse, and More   www.webmd.com

birds stomp on ground worms come up - Google Search   www.google.com

Free Porn Videos & Sex Movies - Porno, XXX, Porn Tube | Pornhub   www.pornhub.com

Butcher's Knot | How to tie a Butcher's Knot using Step-by-Step Animations | Animated Knot...

Home - BBC News   www.bbc.co.uk

B&Q | DIY Products at Everyday Low Prices | DIY at B&Q   www.diy.com

signs that my girlfriend is cheating - Google Search   www.google.com

is my girlfriend cheating on me - Google Search   www.google.com

Frank Ocean - Nights - YouTube   www.youtube.com

Bob Dylan - Make You Feel My Love (Audio) - YouTube   www.youtube.com

YouTube   www.youtube.com

Free Credit Score Report: Credit Monitor | MoneySuperMarket   www.moneysupermarket.com

payday loans repayment - Google Search   www.google.com

what happens in an employee tribunal - Google Search   www.google.com

Free Porn Videos & Sex Movies - Porno, XXX, Porn Tube | Pornhub   www.pornhub.com

wooded walks near me - Google Search   www.google.com

tottenham - Google Search   www.google.com

Mobile Phone Cases and Covers: Amazon.co.uk   www.amazon.co.uk

iphone cases amazon - Google Search   www.google.com

UK News - The latest headlines from the UK | Sky News   news.sky.com

sky news - Google Search   www.google.com

Tue, Apr 1 2019, 3:39 PM

If you want the same as before I have it now

If you want more tho, it'll be later on

📞 PHONE
+44 7590817 - - -
Duration 1 min 14 seconds

Mon, Apr 1 2019, 8:19 PM

Got it. Same place.

📷 iMessage   Send

SATURDAY 30TH MARCH

📞 PHONE
Daniel Carter
Duration 25 min 2 seconds

📞 PHONE
0300 200 1533
Duration 10 seconds

SUNDAY 31ST MARCH

📞 PHONE
Mum
Duration 3 min 52 seconds

📞 PHONE
0300 123 3393
Duration 6 min 33 seconds

MONDAY 1ST APRIL

📞 PHONE
+44 7590817 - - -
Duration 1 min 14 seconds

📞 PHONE
Jess Lloyd
Missed call **(5)**

📞 PHONE
Jess Lloyd
Missed call **(3)**

Mon, Apr 1 2019, 7:08 PM

Are you getting my calls?

Why aren't you answering?

Where are you?

???

I'm getting worried Jack

Where are you?

Tue, Apr 2 2019, 6:20 AM

Jack Norton

What you ringing me for this early Carter?

Dan Carter

There's something I need to tell you

Jack Norton

Fucking hell mate have you pissed the bed or something?

Ato Mizen

I had a missed call too, what's up pal?

Dan Carter

I should ring you all separately but don't think I'll make it through that many calls

I dunno how to say it

Jack Norton

Tell us mate, worrying me now

Dan Carter

I've just got off the phone with Spriggsy girlfriend

Something happened last night

I can't do it like this. I'm going to do a group call. Can you do that here?

PHONE
GROUP CALL - 5 CONNECTED USERS
Duration 5 min 40 seconds

Will Crouch

I'll be at yours in 5 minutes x

Thu, Apr 4 2019, 6:34 PM

What am I supposed to do now Jack?

I'm so hurt

Did you think about me?

You've left me alone

I don't know what to do

What the fuck am I doing, its not like you could ever reply

Fri, Apr 5 2019, 12:57 AM

I've calmed down a bit now but just because you're gone don't think that I can't be in a mood with you. Because I am. I'm so disappointed. There was so much you were supposed to give me Jack. I know that sounds selfish and I don't really mean it, but if I don't say it I know I'll hold onto the anger and thats not how I want to remember you. You were supposed to marry me. We were supposed to have a family. You were supposed to be the father of my children but now you won't. There's so many cant's now Jack. I wish you could have stayed to give me it all.

So many people will be hurting today. I wonder if you thought about that. You probably did. It probably tortured you to think you were going to let people down.

I just wanna hold you so bad

Sat, Apr 6 2019, 10:44 PM

I don't know why I keep texting you but its helping

I'm really feeling it today. I haven't got out of bed. I keep asking myself if I could have stopped it happening.

The worst part is that there probably was something I could have done to stop it and I have to live with that forever

Those last few weeks weren't easy for us. I was probably too hard on you in hindsight and I am so sorry for that.

I keep thinking about everything I said to you and even more about what I didn't say

All those arguments are on repeat in my head, we both know that I'm always right though don't we

I feel guilty for smiling but I just know what you'd be saying if you we're here now

In the UK, approximately 6,000 people a year
will die by suicide and countless more
will attempt to complete suicide.

Notifications   Q

Earlier

 Lauren James, Angie Ferguson
and 103 posted on your wall.   •••

 Angie Ferguson liked a picture
that you are tagged in.   •••

 Jackson Capona tagged you
in a post: "This is never some-   •••

 Simon Bell commented on
your profile picture " We are all   •••

Wed, Apr 10 2019, 1:34 PM

I left the house for the first time today. Honestly, big bad idea. I thought that I should head into town and get some shopping. I haven't been eating much and the fridge is empty.

I thought, just a quick trip to Tesco. Won't take too long. Won't see anyone.

Stepped in the doors and I saw 3 people within the space of like 2 minutes.

Typical.

Can you remember Crouchy's ex?

The one who cheated on him with that boy from Coventry

Well, I looked a state. I had no make up on, my hair was greasy (I'm allowed my boyfriends just killed himself)

She saw me and did this double take. She was probs shocked at how ugly I looked. But she ignored me and let me tell you I've never been happier to be ignored

I wouldn't have known what to say to her if you were with me

Never mind now that you're not

Then it hit me that half of my life was talking about you or something that you were doing, or that we were planning to do together

And now I don't have any of that. Every conversation I start from now on your absence will be a presence

And that's really fucking with me cause I know that other people will think the same thing as soon as they see me

They'll try and dance around the subject of you or even worse talk about you.

I don't know whats worse

Anyway, I managed to get to the bakery aisle. I had planned on getting those donuts that we used to get before Love Island

Those ones with the pink icing and raspberry jam

I got there and they didn't have any and I just started crying

How embarrassing, can you imagine?

I left the trolley in the aisle and just had to get out of there

Jack, I had a breakdown over donuts

So our fridge is still empty, I got a dominos and I guess I'll have to try Tesco's again tomorrow

To The Spriggs Family

With Sympathy

We are truly sorry for your loss. Jack was the brightest,
funniest, and most amazing colleague that
any of us could ever have wished for. Hawkstone will be a
different place without his smiley face around the office floor.
Please accept these flowers and donation from the team here at Hawkstone.

Tue, May 14 2019, 4:29 PM

Hi love, this could be a stupid idea but your lovely Jess has told me to give it a try....She said that she has been trying it and that it has been helping her. Because we have all been struggling, we really have. Sorry, I feel a little silly doing this. What do I say?

We had your funeral yesterday. Sorry, I think you would want to know that. There was lots of people there Jack. All for you, my boy. The church was so full that they had to open the back doors. Just thought you would want to know that. Sorry, I am finding this strange.

The whole day yesterday was a bit of a blur. I didn't feel like I was there fully. All of your friends showed up...the boys looked so smart in their suits.

Tue, May 14 2019, 4:35 PM

Your friend, little Daniel Carter gave me the biggest hug. What a lovely boy he is. I remember when we used to live near him on Aldwych Close and you two were inseparable. You were both always up to some sort of mischief. I miss those days. They flash by so quickly.

He's grown into such a handsome young man. His eyes were so puffy. God, bless him. He kept looking over at your father and I and checking that all of your friends were okay. I think he wanted to speak to me but stopped himself.

I hope he is okay.

Wed, Apr 17 2019, 2:43 AM

Your father is snoring, so there's no chance of me getting to sleep any time soon. I don't feel too tired anyway. I feel drained and a little empty, but not tired. It's a strange feeling.

Does that make sense? I feel like I'm the only person who could know what I mean right now. No one else seems to know.

People keep asking me how I am, or how I'm feeling. I've also been getting a lot of "I can't begin to imagine what you're going through".

I never know what to say to that one.

Wed, Apr 17 2019, 2:55 AM

I usually save the "I'll get there." for people on the outskirts but when your Auntie Leslie asked me last week I had a bit of a breakdown.

It comes in waves, I'm okay some days and others I don't feel like I can get out of bed.

It feels heavy and loud even in the still moments. I can't image how heavy you must have felt during those last few days. I'll try and be strong and carry all that pain for you now, darling.

Wed, Apr 17 2019, 3:03 AM

Sorry, luv. That was supposed to say imagine. It is late. Sorry. I better try and sleep again.

Good night son, I love you x

Thu, Apr 25 2019, 6:48 PM

How could you not tell me?

You arsehole honestly

The bailiffs have just practically knocked the door down and demanded that I pay £8,000

Why didn't you tell me we had that much debt?

I told them about what had happened and they went away but said they'd be in touch again

What am I supposed to do Jack? I can't afford that. I can barely cover the mortgage on my own

I'm doing so much overtime just to cover the costs and I'm doing the best that I can, but I'm drowning Jack.

I don't know how much longer I'll be able to stay here

And it kills me because I don't want to have to give up our house

It's ours and we worked so hard for it

Giving this up and watching someone else live the life we we're suppose to have

A random couple sleeping in our bedroom. Or a girl sitting on our kitchen counter watching her boyfriend cook like we used to on a Sunday morn

Tue, Apr 23 2019, 9:16 AM

Hi son, I found some old pictures yesterday. I sat and looked through them for a few hours with your father. We sat on the floor together and spread them around.

I'm so happy that I took so many pictures!! There was one picture that I took and put in my purse so that I can look at it every time I pay for something.

It's one from your first day of Year 3. Do you remember what happened on that day? Oh god, I remember what hap';fve\iq]0

Oops!! Sorry Jack, I put my phone down to let the dog out and I must have pressed some buttons by mistake. I'm still not the best at this.

Anyway...I remember the morning that we took that picture as if it was yesterday. I was on my lunch break at work when I got the call from Mrs. Thornton. She was the one with the bob wasn't she? God, my heart sunk.

It's a similar feeling to how I've been feeling these past few weeks. I wanted to take away all the embarrassment and hurt and just wrap you up. I just wanted to get to the school as fast as possible and bring those fresh pants to you.

Tue, Apr 23 2019, 10:15 AM

I miss you.

I wish I could hear your voice again. I've been trying to find videos of you from the last few years to try and hear you. But I'm struggling to find any.

Jack, I wish you were here. Just so that I could pick your wet towels up from the bathroom floor. Or be there to help you when you are hungover.

I'm just really missing you, Jack. I wish you we're here but since you're not, I'll carry all that pain that you tried to carry.

I know it feels heavy, it really does but I'll try - for you.

Sat, Apr 27 2019, 6:37 PM

Dan Carter

Anyone up for doing something tonight?

Anyone?

Doesn't have to be drinking? I don't mind, or it can if you boys want. I don't mind.

Just need to get out my place, I'm going crazy ahahah

Ato Mizen

I can't mate. Swamped at work. Still here now. Line managers taking the piss. Soz bud.

Dan Carter

Ah no probs, pal

Jack Norton

Its date night for me mate. She'll boot off I mess with her plans. Might be able to meet up with you after. Could be a bit later though and she'll probs wanna come if were out and about. I'll let you know.

Dan Carter

That's fine mate. Yeah maybe. I was hoping for just a boys night but it's okay I guess.

Crouchy? What you up to?

✓ Read by Ato Mizen, Daniel Carter, Jack Norton and Will Crouch.

The World Health Organisation estimates
that for every 1 person who dies by suicide,
there may be up to 20 others
who will make an attempt on their life.

Sat, Apr 27 2019, 8:04 PM

Hi mate, giving this a try cause Jess told me to. We all know that its wise to do what she says don't we hahaha

She said it helps to chat to you as if you can read what I'm saying and not gonna lie, I've been struggling so I'm up for giving anything a chance right now

I just miss you mate

Wishing you we're here chatting shit

Sat, Apr 27 2019, 8:22 PM

I'm not doing well mate, proper struggling

Keep kicking myself cause I know we talked in those last few weeks about how you weren't doing well but I didn't know how bad it actually was

I think thats the case with it all isn't it, we always try and hide how bad it actually is. Maybe it's shame or just we don't want to admit how bad it is.

Sat, Apr 27 2019, 10:23 PM

Us lads thought you had it all mate. You were the one in the group with the good life. It felt like you had everything and I suppose in some ways you did. A few of us were jealous of you if that's possible, with all good intentions though, never malicious. We just couldn't believe what a lucky bastard you were. You had the new build house with the Barker and Storehouse furniture, the fit girlfriend who actually loved you, the high flying job and a family who were always there. I wanted it, even if it was just a small part. I wanted to be you. I want to be you. I guess it's true what they say isn't it, comparison is the thief of happiness.

I guess that goes to show doesn't it. You don't have a clue what is going on with people. Even those who you are closest to.

I haven't told anyone about what I've been going through.

Tried to reach out to the boys to see if we could catch up a few times, but they've been busy

And I get it, I do. We're all adults and we've got things going on, but it would be good to talk every now and again like we used to

Sat, Apr 27 2019, 10:39 PM

I think thats whats fucking me up, the fact that I don't have someone to talk things through like we used to.

I just feel like I'm alone now if you get me. I know I have the boys but its not the same. Like I can't talk to Crouchy about the stuff we used to. The poor sod hasn't read a book since Of Mice and Men in school. He's not gonna understand whats going on with Russia is he?

And its not even on that level. I feel like we used to just get one another.

Today 11:22 PM

I know that if you were here now I could tell you what has been going on cause I've found it difficult to tell anyone really

Worked up the courage to go and get some help last week

I sat opposite the Doctor and told her that I thought about throwing myself out of the car on the motorway and she asked if I had ever tried the CALM app

The fucking CALM app??

Wed, May 15 2019, 8:11 PM

Morning babe

You should see the weather this morn

It's pouring down, I absolutely cba

I don't know how I'm gonna get to work without getting drenched

Just going to make some brekky and then head in

Speak soon xo

Miss u

Mon, Apr 15 2019, 9:22 AM

Got to work and guess who got drenched

Me

Can't believe I was gonna wear a white shirt too

Pervy Craig from account would have had a field day

Unlucky for him, ey

I'm supposed to be on my lunch at about one today. So I'll check back in with you then. I know you can't reply but I feel better after messaging you.

Wed, May 15 2019, 1:11 PM

Remember when we used to time our lunches so we could ring each other :(

Heading to Pret now for a sandwich

Wed, May 15 2019, 2:13 PM

Gonna try and squeeze in a gym session after work. Mum's been saying I've been going too much but that's stupid. You can't go to the gym too much can you?

Wed, May 15 2019, 7:33 PM

Just making dinner now and the house is sooooo quiet without you. Been playing Queen's greatest hits whilst I cook. I still sit at the table, even without you. It's weird cause I could be slumped on the sofa but it doesn't feel right.

Wed, May 15 2019, 8:07 PM

I'm supposed to be going to your Mum's next week for dinner. She's missing you a lot and she doesn't like me to be alone in our house. Bless her. She really is the cutest.

So excited for Love Island tonight. It's going to be a big episode. Wish you were here to watch it with me. Miss having my legs sprawled all over you.

Thu, May 23 2019, 9:33 PM

Some of the girls have told me that it's not healthy that I message you so often. I kicked off at first, but I do get what they mean. They want the best for me after all. So I'm going to slow down a bit. I don't mean stop completely. I couldn't do that. But I'm becoming a bit obsessive I can feel it. I need to chill a bit. It's not like you can message back. Night. Love you. J x

Hi, me again

Guess that didn't last too long did it? Hahah Something's been playing on my mind since I talked to the girls. They said I'd never get over you if I kept sending you messages like I am. And I've just been thinking like am I ever supposed to get over you? What's the right thing for me to do? Is there a protocol for girlfriends of dead boyfriends to follow? Let's say someone else came along in the next few years who was perfect for me - what would I do then? I'm only 25, Jack. Is that me forever now? A heartbroken widowed fiancé (if that's even a thing). I just don't know. It's all so crazy. Maybe time will tell but right now I don't know. I just can't stop loving you yet.

7:21 AM

Merry Christmas, Jack!

We have all of the family around today and I didn't know when I would get a chance to message. It's the first one without you so it's going to be difficult but we can all get through it. I guess I have to tick off all these dates every year - your birthday, Christmas, the anniversary, New Year's Eve. They'll all come around too fast.

Dinner is at 3. Everyone is coming around like they usually do. Auntie Janet insisted that she do it this year but I refused. It'll keep me busy won't it? Cooking dinner for all sixteen of us Spriggs'. Jess is coming too. I'll leave a space for you at the table next to her, just in case you waltz through the front room door. I've cooked extra pigs in blankets because I know you used to love them. I hope they don't go to waste.

Little Ethan told me that he misses his big strong Uncle Jack yesterday. He was so excited for Santa to come. Bless him. His little face looked up at me in the queue to the Grotto and he said to me that he wishes that you could play with him and his new toys tomorrow.

Sorry, love. Got a little upset writing that one. We're heading to Grandma's now to see everyone for the usual Christmas breakfast. No doubt I'll try and keep myself busy for the rest of the day. Love you lots and miss you more than you'll ever know. Mum x

Thu, Aug 8 2019, 3:49 AM

 Did it hurt?

Symptoms of suicidal behaviour

Any of the following signs could be potential warning signs for suicide.

- Long lasting sadness, mood swings or unexpected rage.
- Sudden calmness.
- Sleep problems.
- Hopelessness about the future.
- Changes in appearance (lack of care).
- Withdrawal - avoiding friends or choosing to be alone.
- Self destructive behaviour (unsafe sex, abusing drugs and alcohol).
- Recent trauma or life crisis (death of a loved one, losing a job, change in financial circumstances).
- Preparing for life after their death (sorting personal circumstances, making a will, giving their personal possessions to loved ones).
- Talking about suicide (50-70% of those considering suicide will try and give a warning sign to someone that they trust.)

Mental health and suicide is a lot more
complicated than these bullet points.
They do however show potential warning signs
that you should know.

about the author

Billy Kelly is a writer from Middlesbrough.
'Messages To Dead Boys' is his debut and is an extension of his work completed during his MA in Creative Writing at Northumbria University. Struggling to come up with an idea for his final project, he was inspired by an event that he witnessed on the way home from a lecture. As he drove across the Tyne Bridge, he noticed a man stood on the edge being coaxed to safety by the police. During the drive home, the idea was born. Whilst researching the statistics for suicide, mental health and mental illness, Billy was shocked by the findings.

Billy wanted to create a piece of literature that identified
warning signs and highlighted the ripple effect
of mental health, suicide and
the lack of mental health services available.

Printed in Great Britain
by Amazon

61362424R00037